# Start Sweating!

## - A KIDS' GUIDE TO BEING ACTIVE -

by Rachelle Kreisman

with illustrations by Tim Haggerty

RED
CHAIR
•PRESS•

Please visit our website at **www.redchairpress.com** for more high-quality products for young readers.

*Start Sweating!*

**Publisher's Cataloging-In-Publication Data**
(Prepared by The Donohue Group, Inc.)

Kreisman, Rachelle, author.

Start sweating! : a kids' guide to being active / by Rachelle Kreisman ; with illustrations by Tim Haggerty.

pages : illustrations ; cm. -- (Start smart: health)

Includes bibliographical references and index.

Summary: There are many ways to be active. Some ways are good for you and keep you healthy. Learn why it is important to be active and discover the fun in sweating for a healthy body.
ISBN: 978-1-937529-65-9 (library hardcover)
ISBN: 978-1-937529-64-2 (paperback)
ISBN: 978-1-937529-87-1 (ebook)

1. Exercise for children--Juvenile literature. 2. Physical fitness for children--Juvenile literature. 3. Exercise. 4. Physical fitness. I. Haggerty, Tim, illustrator. II. Title.

RJ133 .K74 2014

613/.7042                                                                                  2013956241

Illustration credits: p. 1, 3, 4, 7, 8, 11, 12, 13, 20, 22, 23, 25, 26, 27, 29, 30, 31, 32: Tim Haggerty

Photo credits: Cover, p. 4, 5, 6, 7, 8, 9, 10, 12, 13, 15, 16, 19, 20, 21, 23, 24, 25, 26: IStock; p. 5, 11, 14, 15, 18, 24: Dreamstime; p. 13, 17, 24: Shutterstock; p. 13: © B Christopher, Alamy; p.32: Courtesy of the author, Rachel Kreisman

This series first published by:
Red Chair Press LLC          PO Box 333          South Egremont, MA 01258-0333

Printed in the United States of America

1 2 3 4 5 18 17 16 15 14

# Table of Contents

Words in **bold type** are defined in the glossary.

# CHAPTER 1 Why Get Active?

**W**alk, skip, dance, or wiggle. Just get moving! When you move your body, you are being active. It is easy, fun, and good for you. Being active builds strong bones and muscles. It makes your heart stronger too.

Your heart has an important job. It pumps blood to every part of your body. Blood carries **oxygen** and **nutrients** that your body needs to live. When you take care of your heart, it will take care of you.

## TRY THIS!

**Make a fist.** It is about the same size as your heart. Now squeeze your fist tight and then relax it. Try it a few times. That is how your heart works. The walls of your heart are made of muscle. They squeeze and relax to pump blood. In fact, your heart actually acts as two pumps—one on the left side and one on the right.

Being active also fights **obesity**. Obesity is the condition of being very overweight. It can lead to health problems. When you are active, your body burns fat. That helps keep your body at a healthy weight. Having a healthy weight helps prevent illness.

If you are overweight, ask a parent or doctor for advice. Start with a small goal. Exercise a little each day. Build up the amount of time you are active. Every step counts!

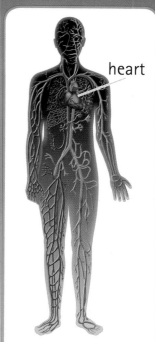

heart

The heart pumps blood to all parts of the body.

If you think being active helps only your body, think again! Being active is good for your mind too. If you are having a bad day, being active may cheer you up. When you exercise, the brain releases chemicals. Those chemicals can make you feel happy. Being fit can also make you feel good about yourself. That should bring a smile to your face.

♥ Being active can make you feel good about yourself.

Maybe you have too much homework or a big test coming up at school. If so, you may have **stress**. Stress is the body's way of reacting when you are worried. That is when exercise comes to the rescue! Exercise can lower stress and make you feel calmer. It can also help you get a better night's sleep. Being active may even help you pay attention in school.

♥ Sleep is good for the body and mind.

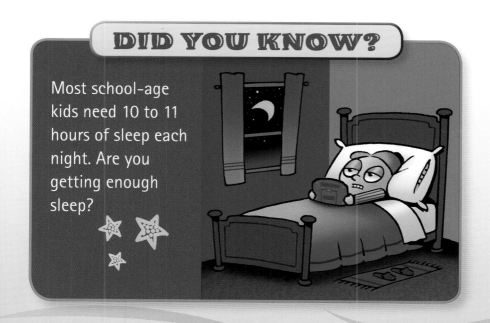

## DID YOU KNOW?

Most school-age kids need 10 to 11 hours of sleep each night. Are you getting enough sleep?

# CHAPTER 2

# All Kinds of Exercise

**K**ids need to be active for at least one hour each day. Don't worry if that sounds like a long time. You can break it up. For example, you can do two 30-minute workouts.

You are probably being active without even knowing it. If you walk or dance, you are being active. If you play tag or catch, you are doing something active. Cleaning your room also counts. (And no, watching television does not count!)

## FUN FACT!

**Bones! Bones! Bones!** Where are more than half of a person's bones found? In the hands and feet! Each hand has 27 bones. Each foot has 26 bones.

Hand = 27 bones

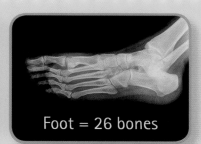

Foot = 26 bones

Not all exercise is the same. People need different kinds of activity. **Aerobic** (ai-ROH-bik) **exercise** gets your heart pumping faster. Some exercise makes your bones stronger. Other activities make your muscles stronger. You can also exercise to make your body more **flexible**. That makes it easier to stretch and bend.

♥ There are lots of ways to keep your heart active and have fun too.

♥ Aerobic exercise gets your heart beating faster and makes you sweat.

Aerobic activities make your heart stronger. Try playing sports or jumping rope. Run, dance, or ride your bike. Those activities take a lot of energy. They get your heart pumping faster and make you **sweat**.

During a heart-pumping activity, you breathe harder and faster. You will not be able to sing. If you are moving very fast, talking may be difficult too. You may only be able to say a few words at a time. Just. Like. *Huff*. This. *Puff*.

Why do you huff and puff during exercise? Lungs take in oxygen from the air. Your body needs more oxygen during exercise. When you breathe faster and harder, your lungs take in more oxygen. That is why your heart speeds up. By beating faster, your heart can pump blood faster. The blood carries more oxygen to your muscles. The word *aerobic* means "with air" or "with oxygen."

## TRY THIS!

**Heartbeats!** At rest, a child's heart beats about 90 times each minute. Find out how fast your heart is beating. You will need a watch or clock with a secondhand.

Turn one of your arms so you are looking at your inner wrist. Place the fingers of your other hand on your inner wrist. Press down with your fingers. Do you feel a beat? That is your **pulse**.

Take your pulse for one minute.

Count the number of beats you feel in one minute. Try taking your pulse when you are at rest. Then take your pulse after you exercise. Did you notice a difference? Why do you think that happens?

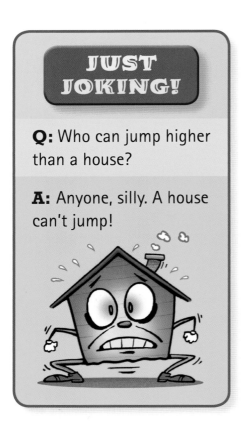
Jump for your bones! They are still growing. Exercise helps build strong bones. To work, the exercise has to put force on your bones. That often happens when you are on your feet carrying your body weight. Run, jump, and hop. Try playing soccer, tennis, or basketball. The force of hitting your feet against the ground helps your bones grow and get stronger.

♥ Jumping rope helps build strong bones.

What exercises are good for you, but don't help bones? Swimming and biking. That is because they don't put force on your bones. Those activities are still great for your body. They make your heart and muscles stronger.

♥ Swimming does not put force on your bones. It makes your heart and muscles strong.

## DID YOU KNOW?

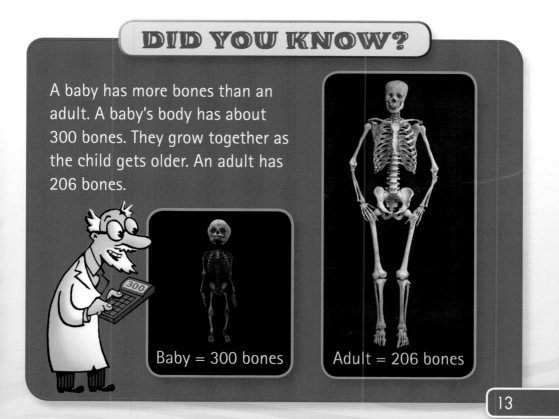

A baby has more bones than an adult. A baby's body has about 300 bones. They grow together as the child gets older. An adult has 206 bones.

Baby = 300 bones

Adult = 206 bones

♥ Swinging across monkey bars makes your arm muscles stronger.

Don't move a muscle! Just kidding. Even if you try really hard, you won't be able to do it. The muscles in your body are always moving. Some muscles keep your lungs breathing. Others keep your heart pumping. Muscles even help move food through the body.

Now go ahead and show off your arm muscles. The muscles you control are called **skeletal muscles**. They are attached to your **skeleton**. When you use those muscles, you make them stronger. Ride a bicycle. Walk up and down hills. Do sit-ups. See how many push-ups you can do. Swing across monkey bars. Keep it up and you will be stronger in no time.

Can you bend down and touch your toes? When you are flexible, you can easily stretch and bend. Being flexible can keep you from getting hurt during exercise. Help your body become more flexible by doing stretches. You can also try yoga, martial arts, and gymnastics.

♥ Doing stretches and becoming flexible can keep you from getting hurt during exercise.

# CHAPTER 3

# Safety First

**Ouch.** Getting hurt can really spoil a good time. But there are many ways to stay safe while being active. When you keep the injuries away, you will have more time to play. Hooray!

Dress in clothes that allow you to move freely. Try not to wear cotton against your skin. It stays wet when you sweat. Choose fabrics such as merino wool and polyester blends. They wick sweat away from the body and keep you dry. Make sure you wear the right shoes too. Sneakers are often a good choice.

## DID YOU KNOW?

A good helmet should fit snugly. If the helmet is loose, it can slip to one side. The helmet also needs to sit straight on your head and cover your forehead. It should rest about an inch above your eyebrows. Fasten the chin strap tightly, but not so it hurts. If you can fit a finger between the buckle and your chin, the strap is just right.

For many sports, wearing safety gear is important. Always wear a helmet when you ride a bike or do other wheel sports. A helmet protects your head and brain during a fall. Wear gloves to protect your hands. Also wear kneepads, elbow pads, and wrist guards if you skate or ride a scooter.

Special gear may be needed for other sports too. Check with a parent or coach to find out what to wear.

Always wear the right gear to protect yourself when playing sports.

The sun is shining. The birds are chirping. Do you hear that? Nature is calling you! It's time to play outside and breathe in some fresh air. Before you do, prepare for the sun. Some of the sun's rays are harmful. They can cause damage to your skin and eyes.

If you are out in the sun, wear sunscreen. It should have an **SPF** (sun protection factor) of 30 or higher. Rub it in where your skin is showing. Wear a hat and sunglasses too. Move to the shade or go inside to take breaks.

♥ Wear sunscreen, a hat, and sunglasses to stay safe in the sun.

*Brrrr.* It is c-c-cold outside. Don't let that stop you from having fun. Keep warm by dressing in layers. Avoid wearing cotton against your skin. Put on a jacket too. If you start to get warm, don't sweat it— you can remove one or more layers. Make sure to wear gloves and a hat too.

If it's snowing, wear boots and waterproof pants. Now that you are bundled up, there is one more thing— sunscreen. The snow reflects the sun's rays so you can still get a sunburn. Put sunscreen on your face. Use lip balm with SPF to protect your lips. Now you are ready to go!

♥ When it is cold, keep warm by dressing in layers. If you start to get warm, you can remove a layer.

You are dressed and ready to move. Wait a minute! You seem to be forgetting something. Here is a hint—it is wet and starts with the letter *w*. If you guessed *water*, you are correct! Before

♥ Drink water before, during, and after exercise—even if you are not thirsty.

you get moving, drink some water. Drink before, during, and after exercise. Remember to have lots of water—even if you are not thirsty. Your body needs water to keep cool. The more you sweat, the more you need to drink.

**JUST JOKING!**

**Q:** How do star athletes keep cool during a game?

**A:** They play near their fans!

Are you ready to get moving? Not so fast! First, you need to warm up. Start with five to 10 minutes of light exercise. Light exercise is slow and gentle on your body. You can breathe normally. You are able to talk to a friend. You will not be sweating. Any gentle activity is fine. Just remember to increase your speed slowly. That gets your body ready for faster activity.

♥ Warm up slowly before faster exercise.

## DID YOU KNOW?

When your body gets too hot, it releases sweat. The wet stuff is mostly made up of water. It leaves your body through tiny holes in your skin. The tiny holes are called **pores**. When sweat first leaves your pores, it is a liquid. It hits the air and turns into **water vapor**. Then poof—the heat is removed and your body cools down!

## CHAPTER 4 | Getting Started

**N**ow you know why being active is good for you. You also know how to stay safe. Next is the fun part. Get moving! Nothing is stopping you. Try different activities to see which you like best. No matter where you are, you can make exercise a part of each day.

At home, shut off the television and step away from the computer. You can do it! Now you have more time to get moving. Do you feel healthier already? If not, turn on some music and move around. Do sit-ups. If you have stairs, climb them. Amaze your family by cleaning your room or helping with chores around the house.

### DID YOU KNOW?

Stay inside during a thunderstorm. If you can hear thunder, lightning is close by. It is not safe to play outside.

Go outside if you can. Spin a hula hoop. Jump rope. Play a game of catch with a friend. Bounce a ball. Ride a bike. Walk up and down hills. See if you can run, skip, hop, and then walk some more. Play hopscotch.

Don't let snow or a little rain slow you down. If it snows, go sledding. Build a snowman. If you feel too cold, take breaks by going inside to warm up. A rain shower should not get in your way either. Just remember to put on your boots and raincoat first.

Try joining a team if you like to play sports. Not only are team sports good exercise, they will also help you learn to follow rules. Plus, you can make new friends. Try soccer, T-ball, or softball.

What's that you say? You don't like team sports. No problem. You have many other choices. Try yoga, tennis, or martial arts. Take swim lessons. In addition to being active, you will learn water safety. You may also like gymnastics, dance, or figure skating.

tennis

💜 Try different types of exercise to see what you like best.

dance

martial arts

❤ Sneak exercise into your day, try taking the stairs instead of the elevator.

*Shh!* Here is a little secret you might not know. You can sneak exercise into your day. If you are sitting for a long time, take a break. Get up and stretch. Sit down in your chair and stand up. Repeat a few times. Step in place while waiting in line. Use the stairs instead of an elevator. Walk the long way to get to where you need to go. Last, but not least, have fun!

## DID YOU KNOW?

Experts say kids should play more than one kind of sport. Kids who do might be less likely to get hurt. Playing only one sport can put too much work on the same muscle groups. For example, you might overuse your arm if you play tennis. If you switch to soccer, you give your arm a rest.

Hey! Are you still here? Reading this book is great, but you should get some exercise. Go on now. Be like a cow and get *moo*-ving! Actually, cows really don't move that much. You can probably move much more. In that case, just be yourself. You will be fine as long as you are being active.

♥ Exercising with friends can make you feel happy.

# What You Can Do!

How many of these rules do you follow?
Count the number of things you do.
See how you score below.

## You . . .

1. are active for at least 60 minutes each day.
2. try new activities to see what you like best.
3. drink water before, during, and after exercise.
4. put on sunscreen and sunglasses when in the sun.
5. wear the right clothes and shoes for each activity.
6. dress in layers and gloves when it is cold outside.
7. wear a helmet when you do wheel sports.
8. do aerobic exercise to make your heart stronger.
9. exercise to make your bones and muscles stronger.
10. stretch to make your body more flexible.

## If you answered "yes" to . . .

* **eight or more** — Great job being active!

* **five to seven** — You are almost there.

* **one to four** — Keep trying. You can do it!

# Glossary

**aerobic exercise:** exercise that increases the body's need for oxygen

**flexible:** able to bend easily

**nutrients:** the good things found in food that people need to grow and live

**obesity:** the condition of being very overweight

**oxygen:** a gas in the air that people need to live

**pores:** tiny holes in the skin

**pulse:** a regular beat caused by the heart squeezing and releasing blood

**skeleton:** all the bones in the body

**skeletal muscles:** the muscles that people control

**SPF (sun protection factor):** a measure of how long a person can stay in the sun without getting a sunburn

**stress:** the body's way of reacting when a person is worried

**sweat:** to give off moisture through the skin's pores

**water vapor:** water in the form of a gas

# What Did You Learn?

See how much you learned about being active. Answer *true* or *false* for each statement below. Write your answers on a separate piece of paper.

**1** Being active can help you sleep better at night. True or false?

**2** Your heart pumps blood all around your body. True or false?

**3** Sweat is the body's way of staying warm. True or false?

**4** Kids don't need to wear sunscreen in the winter. True or false?

**5** Running and jumping builds strong bones. True or false?

Answers: 1. True, 2. True, 3. False (Sweat is the body's way of staying cool.), 4. False (Kids need to wear sunscreen when playing in the snow. Snow reflects the sun's rays.), 5. True.

# For More Information

## Books

Bailey, Jacqui. *What Happens When You Move?* The Rosen Publishing Group, Inc., 2009.

Gray, Shirley Wimbish. *Exercising for Good Health* (Living Well). The Child's World, 2004.

Green, Jen. *Muscles* (Your Body and Health). Aladdin Books Ltd, 2006.

Hewitt, Sally. *My Heart and Lungs* (My Body). QEB Publishing, 2008.

Showers, Paul. *Hear Your Heart* (Let's-Read-and-Find-Out Science). HarperCollins Publishers Inc., 2001.

## FUN FACT!

**Babe Ruth** (1895–1948) was a famous American baseball player. He had his own way of staying cool during games. What did he do? He kept a chilled lettuce leaf under his baseball cap!

# Web Sites

American Heart Association: www.heart.org

CDC: BAM! Body and Mind:
http://www.cdc.gov/bam/activity

KidsHealth.org: Be a Fit Kid:
http://kidshealth.org/kid/stay_healthy/fit/fit_kid.html

Let's Move: http://www.letsmove.gov/kids

Texas Heart Institute: Project Heart:
http://www.texasheartinstitute.org/ProjectHeart

**Note to educators and parents:** Our editors have carefully reviewed these web sites to ensure they are suitable for children. Web sites change frequently, however, and we cannot guarantee that a site's future contents will continue to meet our high standards of quality and educational value. You may wish to preview these sites and closely supervise children whenever they access the Internet.

# Index

# About the Author

Rachelle Kreisman has been a children's writer and editor for many years. She wrote hundreds of classroom magazines for *Weekly Reader*. Those issues included health topics about nutrition, illness prevention, sports safety, and fitness. When Rachelle is not writing, she enjoys being active. She likes taking walks, hiking, biking, kayaking, and doing yoga.